My Cat
Mrs Christmas

Adrian Mitchell
Illustrated by Sophy Williams

Dolphin

To my big brother Jimmy
and his family, with love
A.M.

Published in paperback in 1999
First published in Great Britain in 1998
by Orion Children's Books
a division of the Orion Publishing Group Ltd
Orion House
5 Upper St Martin's Lane
London WC2H 9EA

Text copyright © Adrian Mitchell 1998
Illustrations copyright © Sophy Williams 1998

A catalogue record for this book is available from the British Library
Printed in Italy
Designed by Dalia Hartman

It was Christmas morning.
The moon was still in the window.
Jimmy and I had opened our stockings.

Jimmy was trying to read an Annual.
I was playing my drum and singing.
We were both full of excitement and chocolate.

Wilfred, our brave fox-terrier, galloped in, barking.
Was there a fire? Or a burglar? Or a terrible monster?

In came Mum and Dad, smiling in their dressing-gowns.
Mum was holding a dark furry ball.

She put the ball gently on Jimmy's bed.
It opened itself out into a tabby kitten.

The kitten yawned.
It was about as small as a teacup.
"What shall we call her?" asked Dad.

We all stood round her, thinking with our brains.
Then I had the brightest idea of my whole life.
"Mrs Christmas!" I said. "We'll call her Mrs Christmas!"
I picked her up carefully and touched noses with her.
"Your name is Mrs Christmas," I said.
The whole family agreed, even Jimmy.

At Christmas dinner, she sat on the table.
She sipped from her own blue bowl of cream.
Wilfred stood by the door, like a soldier on guard.

Mrs Christmas grew bigger.
Soon she was up to mischief.
She clawed the sofa and scratched up important letters.

She climbed on the mantelpiece and mewed at the mirror.
Then she turned round and jumped on top of Dad's head.
He walked about wearing her like a tabby hat.

Mrs Christmas was cheeky to Wilfred.
She walked underneath him when he least expected it.

We made her a soccer ball out of silver paper.
She loved to chase it all over the hall.

Spring came, and Mrs Christmas explored the garden.
Mostly she stayed in our old apple tree, laughing at Wilfred.

She grew bigger and bigger.
Soon she was as big as your head and a fat weight to carry.

One morning, when we came down to breakfast,
Mum and Dad shushed us.
Mrs Christmas was in her basket, purring.
Six skinny kittens were drinking milk from her.

We watched them for a long time.
Their eyes hadn't opened yet.
Wilfred growled if we went too near.

Soon the kittens were running races and mountaineering.
They held wrestling matches.
They treated poor Wilfred as a climbing frame.
"It's like living in a jungle," said Mum.

Mrs Christmas decided to tame her kittens.
She took command of an old cardboard box.
She chased her kittens into it.

When they needed exercise, she nudged them out of the box.
She marched them up and down, into the garden and back again.

As she marched her kittens around, she said proudly:
"I am Mrs Christmas."
She spoke in the language of tabby cats.

People sometimes ask: "Why is she called Mrs Christmas?"
If Jimmy doesn't stop me, I tell them.
I say: "It was me that called her Mrs Christmas.
You see – it was Christmas morning.
The moon was still in the window…"
And I tell them the rest of this story, all the way down to

THE END